When Fred The Snake Got Squished, And Mended

Peter Cotton
Jan 2014

Written by

Peter B. Cotton

illustrated by

Bonnie Lemaire

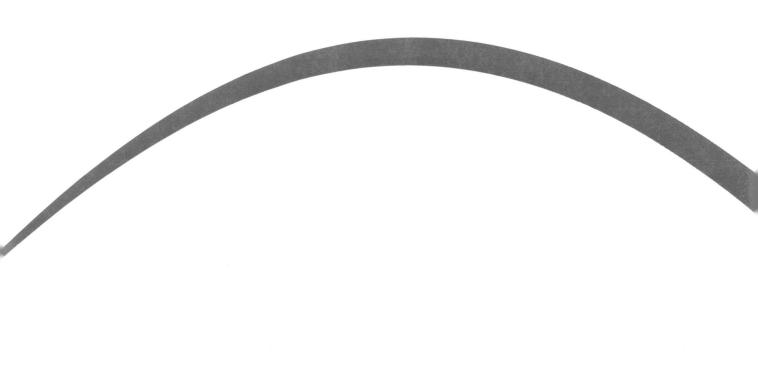

This Book Belongs To:

Iza and Cy Nahas

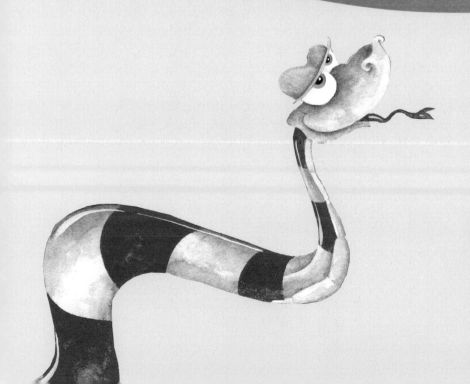

"Fred-Fred" was written
many years ago for my children,
Andrew and Nicola. It is now published
and dedicated to their wonderful children,
Alexandra, Charlotte, Isobelle,
Perdita and Jack.

One day, as we sat down to tea,
a package came, addressed to me;
the sort with holes in it, which leave
air inside, for pets to breathe.

There, lying on a leafy bed
was my gift, a snake called Fred.
A note said "love from Jungle Jim,
be sure and take good care of him".

Fred was his name, but soon, instead,
we'll have to call him 'Fred-dash-Fred',
for I'll tell you how we made ends meet,
when he lost his head while crossing the street.

Fred came from a steamy forest spot,
where even winter days are hot,
the home of hairy beasts that go oink-oink,
and drop things on your head, boink-boink.

It's a swampy place with lots of squelch,
the only noise a muffled belch,
of a nearby rhino in the mud,
chewing the primeval cud.

Such a rush when we first went out,
with noise and cars all dashing about.

Fred was jungle-trained a treat,
but, could he cross a busy street

When we came to cross the road,
Fred quite forgot his Forest Code.

He thought the barber's stripy pole
was a friendly snake, but, oh my soul

Fred dashed across with never a glance
into the path of an ambulance.

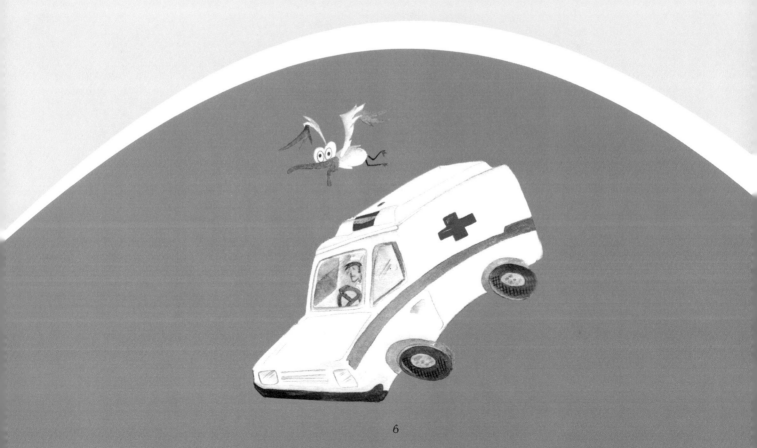

With a horrible SCREECH, it wasn't his fault,
the driver did his best to halt,
and, like most snakes,
Fred had no brakes.

Before my eyes poor hurrying Fred
was CUT IN TWO...he scarcely bled
for in snakes blood a something flows
to stop them leaking when they're squoze.

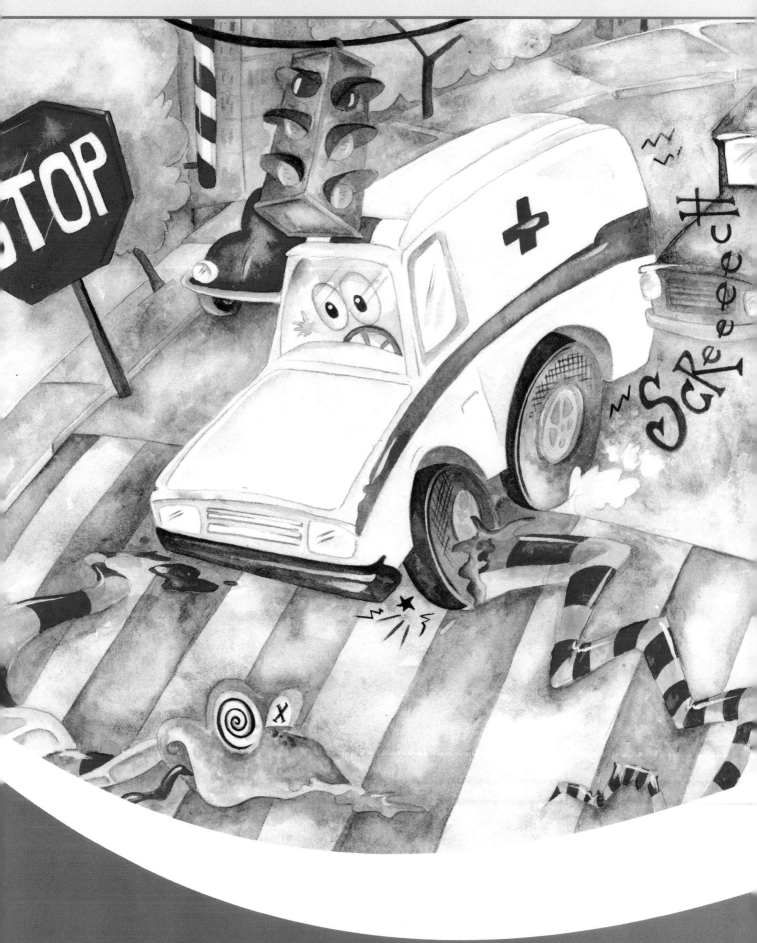

The driver jumped down, from his pack he took
his first-aid kit and his first-aid book —
in the index found "for SNAKES DIVIDED
use the longest splint provided."

But even that was much too small,
The two Fred parts were far too tall.

We had to call for further aid,
and pretty soon the Fire-Brigade
had Fred all comfy on their ladder
(they'd once been called to a fractured adder).

With Police cars leading them ahead,
they dashed through all the lights at red,
and halted at the Hospital gate.
Oh, will they have to operate?

Doctors came and called a Vet,
not a case they often get,
They sounded his chest and made him sick
by poking his throat with a long flat stick.
They put him on trolleys (he needed four),
and wheeled him through the X-Ray door.

I saw the specialist doctor frown
as he put poor Fred-Fred's X-rays down.
"We'll have to do our best to sew
these ends together, but you know
(to the nurses gathered round he said)
I'll need a special sort of thread
full of twist and curl and bend
to make a proper snake-proof mend.

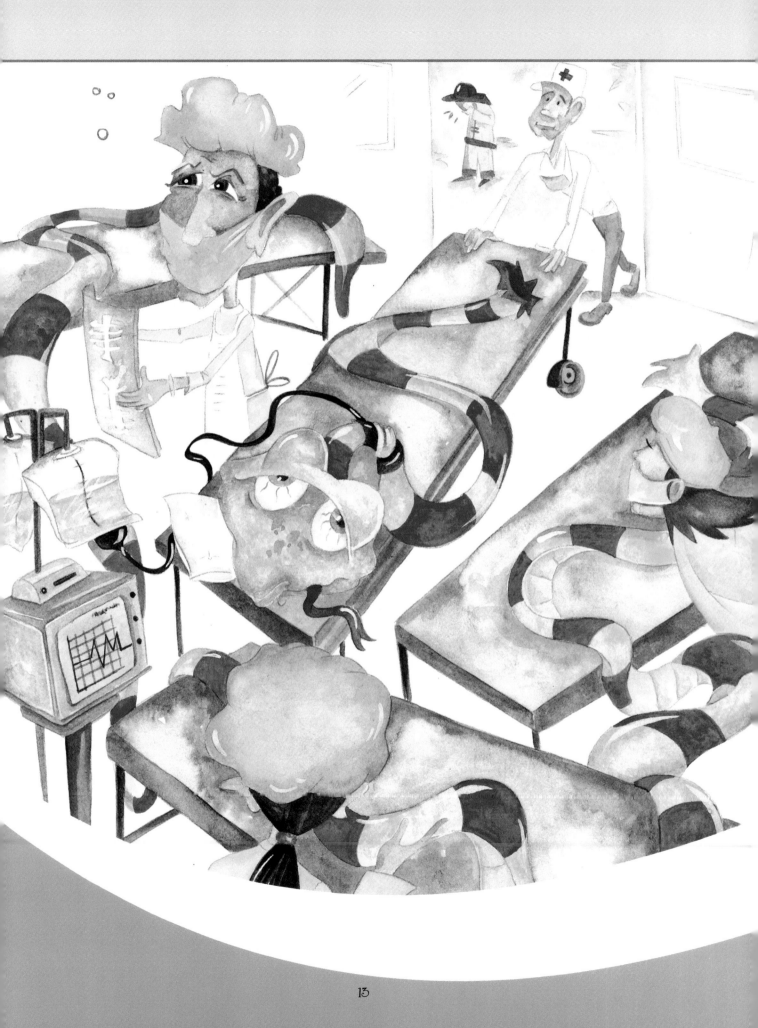

This thread comes only from the leaf
of a certain bush which grows beneath
large rhinos. But, who will dare
disturb that wild beast in his lair?"

"Volunteers, please give your names."

Suddenly I thought of James,
who enjoys, so one supposes,
hunting fierce Rhi-nos-cer-oses.

So we wrote post-haste to Jim,
in CATIPALS, informing him,
of the needs of Fred, or rather Freds,
for the parts now lay in separate beds.

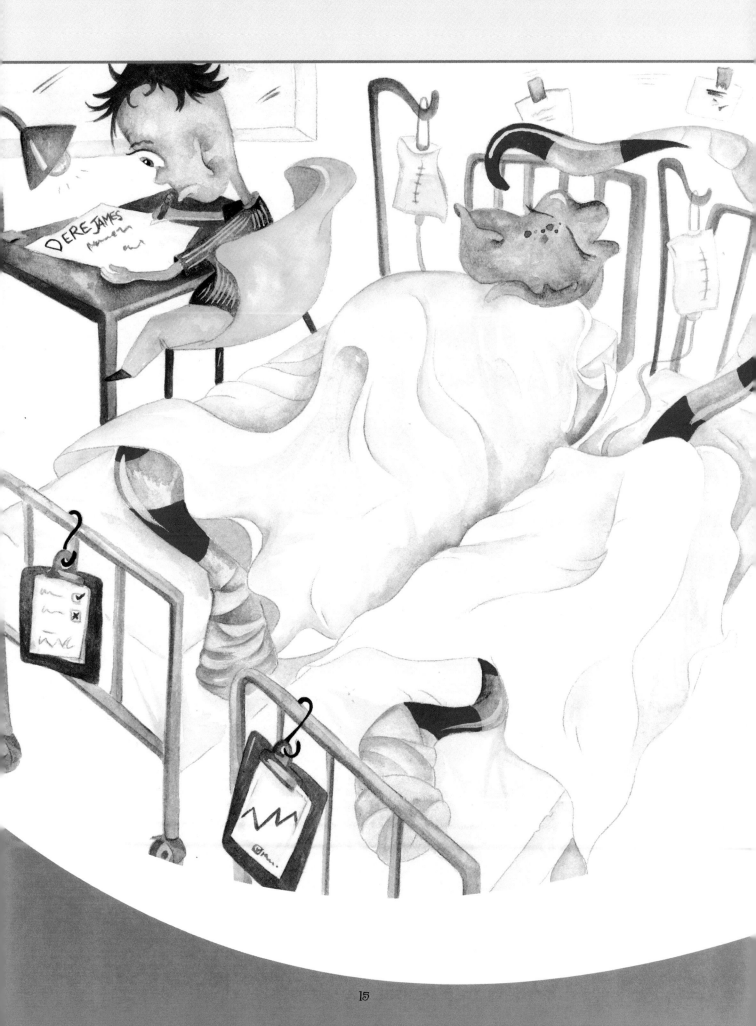

Jim read the note, but his mortal dread
was waking rhinos in their beds.

But he bravely started out to hike
(he'd punctured his exploring bike)
and laid his bait, an open box
of rhino's favourite sort of chocs.

Woken from his dreamy coma
by a birthday sort aroma,
the rhino staggered to his feet,
and shambled off towards his treat

From his hiding-place, neck-deep in slime,
Jim, picking the auspicious time,
stretched out his hand and with it caught,
the leaf our Fred-Fred's doctor sought.

With loving care he packed it in
his jungle-issue sandwich tin,
and sealed it with a Forest stamp.

A monkey swung it back to camp
and sent it seagull-post that day
across the seas where Fred-Fred lay.

19

The doctor then, immediately,
or, rather, when he'd had his tea,
prepared the thread and started sewing
Fred-Fred's coming to his going.

The brave snake didn't cry or ouch
on the operating couch.

Then doctor asked the nurse to bring
the special snakey sort of sling
which helps in bendy types of healing.
Soon Fred was slung up from the ceiling!

Within a week, with stitches out,
Fred found that he could twist about;
He did his exercises so
they soon pronounced him fit to go.

Fred kept a careful hold of me,
as we hurried home for tea,
of jelly, cream, and beans on toast,
the things that mended Freds like most.

Then we wrote brave Jim a letter
saying Fred was so much better,
and thanked him for the jungle trip
to provide our snake with a sort of zip.

Then Fred washed, put on his jamas —
just the leg part, not the armas —
and curled up, having said his prayers,
in his box beneath the stairs.

As he fell asleep I heard Fred say
"It's been a very trying day;
Tomorrow, when I'm on the road
I won't forget my Crossing Code."

And nor will you, that's my advice,
Lest you spell your name with a hyphen, twice.

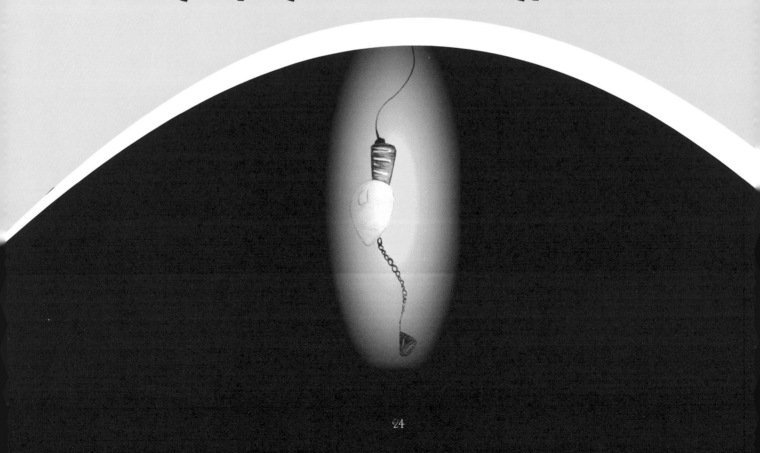

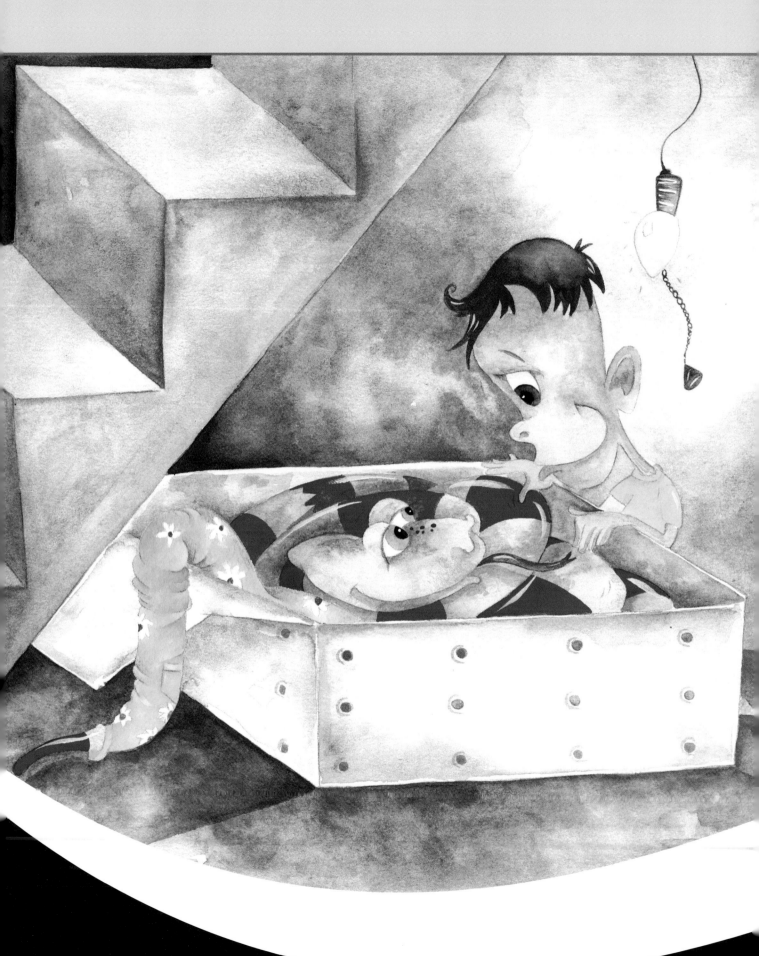

 **Dr. Peter Cotton** was born in Herefordshire, England, where his father was a country physician. He was educated at Cambridge University and at St. Thomas Hospital Medical School (London), and graduated as a doctor in 1963. He eventually became a Gastro-enterologist, and ran a leading department at The Middlesex Hospital in London, before moving to USA in 1986 to become Professor of Medicine at Duke University in North Carolina. In 1994, he moved again to set up the Digestive Disease Center at the Medical University of South Carolina in Charleston. He recently retired from clinical work but continues part-time in research and teaching. He has written many medical textbooks, almost 1000 papers, and recently published his memoirs entitled *The Tunnel at the End of the Light: My Endoscopic Journey in Six Decades* (details at www.peterbcotton.com). All proceeds from that book go to support post-graduate training in advanced endo-scopic procedures.

This children's book, often nicknamed "Fred-Fred" by young readers, was written for his own children almost 40 years ago, but was published only recently after he found an excellent illustrator. He now enjoys reading it to his grandchildren. Dr. Cotton jokes, "American children (and some adults) giggle when they hear my name, assuming that I was named after a rabbit. In vain I tell them that Beatrix Potter wrote about Peter Rabbit, Flopsy, Mopsy, Benjamin Bunny and Cottontail, not about Peter Cottontail. My middle name is Benjamin!" He is working on sequels called *When Fred the Snake Goes to School*, and *When Jungle Jim Came to Visit Fred the Snake*.

Check out Peter Cotton's *Fred the Snake* facebook page, and his website at www.petercottontales.com.

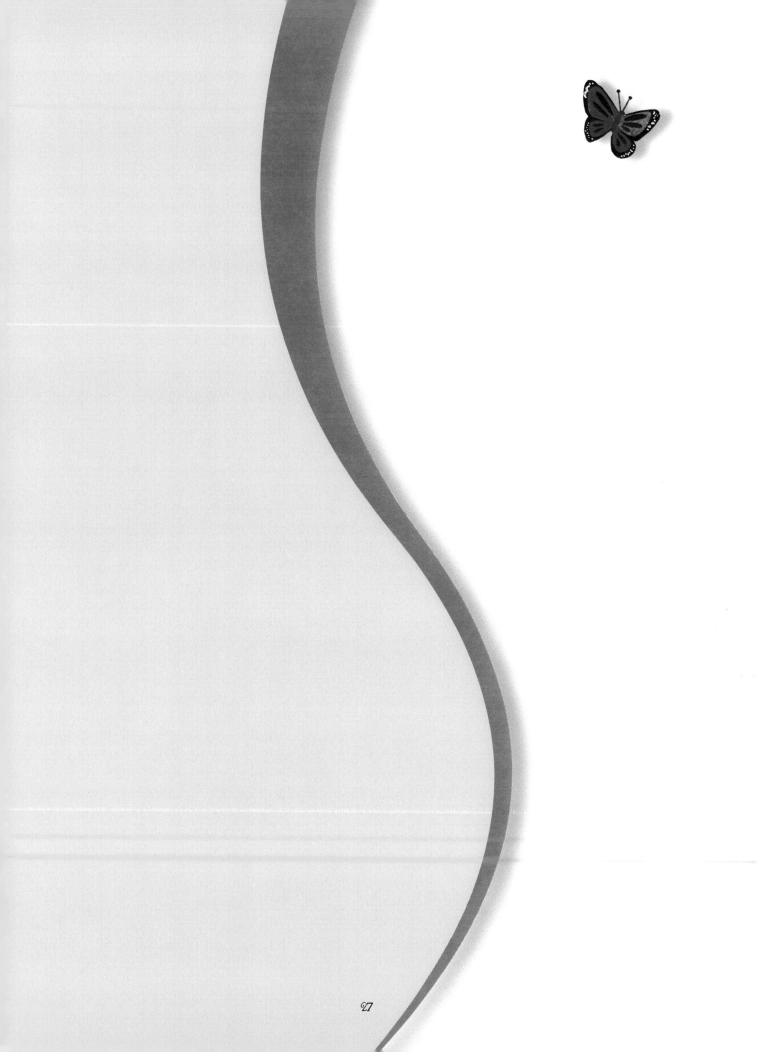

CPSIA information can be obtained
at www.ICGtesting.com
Printed in the USA
LVIW02n0339130813
347584LV00001B